Wisdom in the MEOW

By Kimberly Fleck

Illustrated by Jessica Aranda

Halo
PUBLISHING
INTERNATIONAL

ISBN: 978-1-63765-050-9
LCCN: 2021911321

Halo Publishing International, LLC
8000 W Interstate 10, Suite 600
San Antonio, Texas 78230
www.halopublishing.com

Printed and bound in the United States of America

To animals everywhere. May we love them.

Respect them. And protect them.

Spiral up, in the MEOW!

Hi, my name is Wu Kitty. I am a sassy orange rescue girl from New York City.

4

This is my silly sidekick, the white dog with the brown spots. His real name is Finnegan. I call him Finn for short.

Hi there, I'm Finn. I'm a sweet, lovable, happiness-maker rescued from South Carolina.

STAYING IN BALANCE CAN BE A TRICKY THING TO DO

Finn and I have noticed that humans appear to struggle a great deal with this. They seem to have a difficult time being in the now, or as I call it, being in the "MEOW."

ANIMALS DON'T HAVE THIS PROBLEM

We live in the moment. We are present.
We are not worrying about the future
or dwelling on the past.

When you are in the MEOW, you are in the NOW. You are in the moment and you will begin to pay much closer attention to the world around you and the world inside of you.

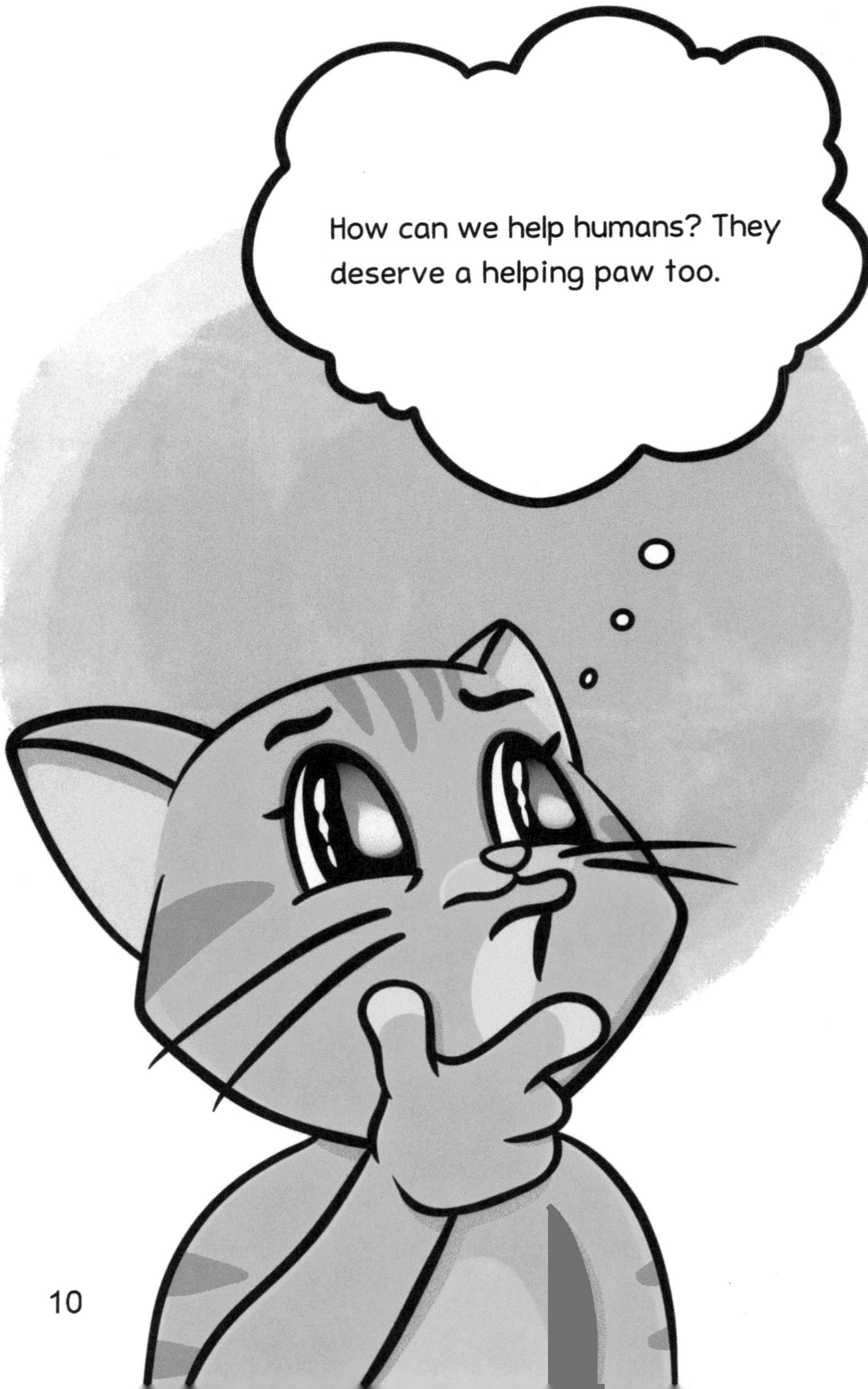
How can we help humans? They deserve a helping paw too.

We decided to share some of Wu's wisdom in order to help you live more in the MEOW.

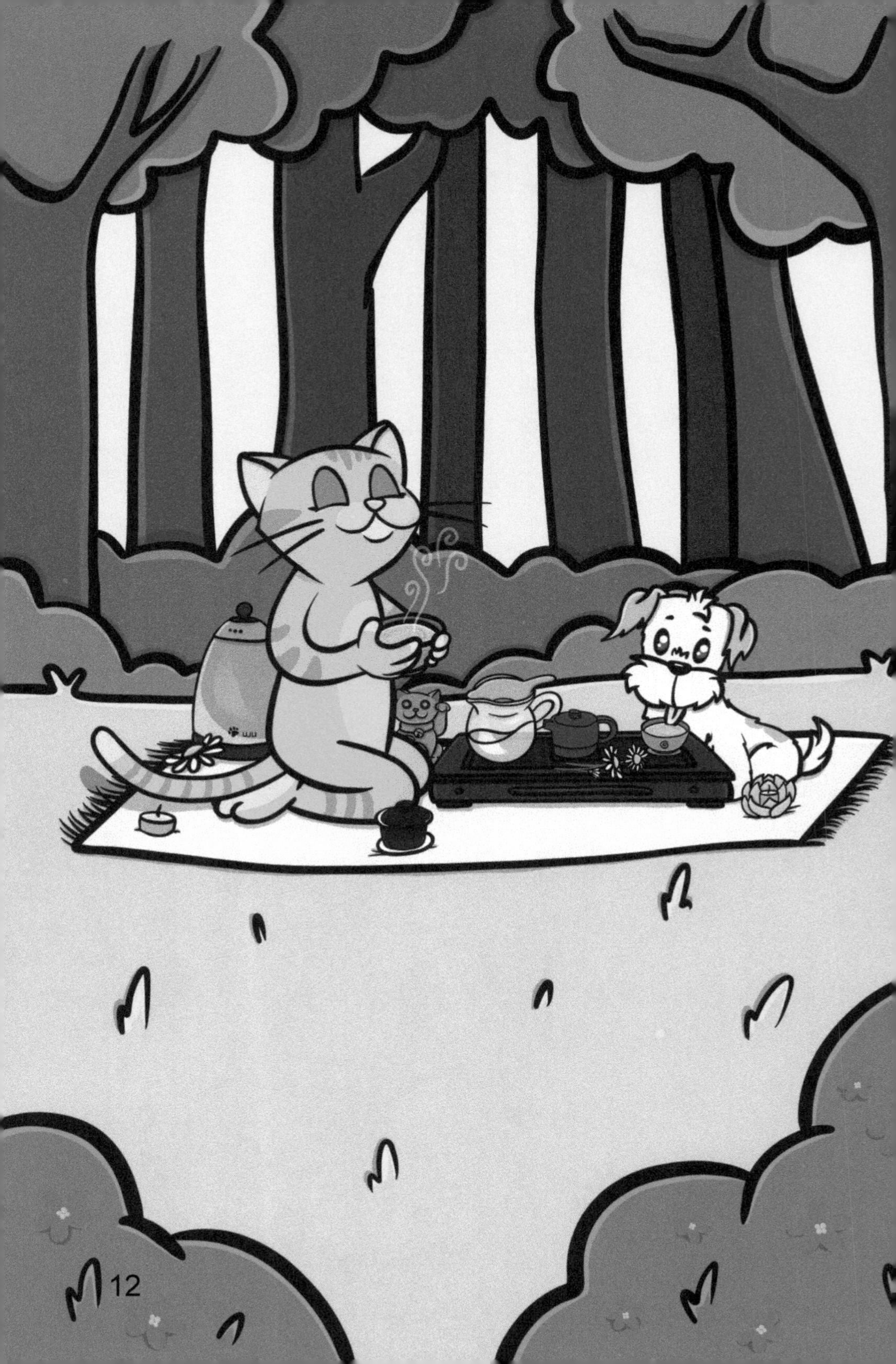

Finding happiness and gratitude in the moment is easy once you begin to look, smell, feel and listen more closely. When we begin to practice slowing down, we become more grounded and centered. Finn and I do this each day with a morning tea ceremony. We focus on the smells and taste and set our intentions. We focus on what we want and not on what we don't want. Most importantly, we send positive vibes and gratitude to people and animals around the world and to those in the heavens.

Finn loves the smell of the ocean air. The air brings him clarity and the sand grounds him. His entire being is full of joy.

I love the smell of what comes out of the ocean...SALMON!

This is what it means
to live your best life!
To live in the MEOW.

SOUNDS CAN BRING US BACK TO THE PRESENT AND KEEP US FOCUSED

16

The sounds of nature and music are wonderful ways to connect and help us to stay in the MEOW. Being in the MEOW is far from boring. It can spark creativity, adventure and a zest for life.

Sound healing, audiobooks and podcasts are all brilliant ways to take us on exciting adventures, exploring new ideas and exotic lands and bringing us a sense of joy and serenity while still being present in the core of our being.

MOTHER EARTH IS OUR GREATEST TEACHER

Place your paws on the grass or in the dirt and feel that connection to the Earth below you; you will immediately begin to feel better. That feeling of being connected with nature is powerful and healing. Do this as often as you can. You can thank us later.

ENGAGE IN
LAUGHTER AND SHENANIGANS

Laugh long and hard. Do this every day.
Multiple times a day.

Laughter is always in the MEOW and will
keep you connected to your internal joy.

Engage in harmless shenanigans. They will
keep you connected to your younger self
and to your best mates.

DO WHAT YOU LOVE

Be aware of what brings you joy and do that as often as you can. If it's not connected to your occupation, be sure to incorporate it into your daily activities. That which brings us joy keeps us healthy, happy and on purpose. When you are on purpose, you are in the MEOW.

MEDITATION IN MOTION

Practice quiet activities that promote stillness within and yet still allow you to move your body. I love qigong and tai chi.

Finn loves yoga, especially Downward Dog.

DIFFERENT ANGLES

When viewing the world around you, it comes down to one main thing, perspective. We see things from many different angles.

If you look at something from above or from below, it looks different. The same holds true when you're looking at it from one side to the other. Your view is often just one of many. Try to remember that.

When you are experiencing "Monkey Mind".

Just give the monkeys a job. They will thank you for it.

FORGIVE
IT'S TOO HEAVY
FOR YOU TO CARRY

When you forgive, it allows you to heal. Whenever you can, try to send love to those whom you believe have wronged you. This allows you to feel lighter. By letting the past go and freeing yourself from the pain and sadness connected to a person or a particular event, you are setting yourself free. You are able to live in the MEOW and in joy. Say goodbye to the past for good.

I AM FORGIVING
– I AM FORGIVEN

We all make mistakes and that includes you.

We can't change the past. We can only learn from it. You are growing.

Realize that you are a different being now and focus on being present.

Live in the MEOW and celebrate YOU in each moment!

WE ALL BRING SOMETHING OF VALUE TO THE WORLD CELEBRATE THAT!

Embrace your uniqueness and differences and celebrate them in others. In each moment, we can learn and teach. We can embrace and empower. We can love and connect. All paws on deck, my friends, because when you're in the MEOW, you can make the world a better place for EVERYONE!

TRUE LISTENING IS A VERY POWERFUL TOOL

Be present when you are with others. Be an active listener. You will find your connections to others become more meaningful. Listening provides the opportunity to internalize information and feel directly connected to another soul's wisdom and experiences.

TREAT YOURSELF THE WAY YOU WOULD TREAT OTHERS

Be kind to yourself. Practice "Pawsitive" self-talk. It may sound silly, but practicing "Pawsitive" self-talk can help to keep us in the moment, in gratitude and feeling healthy.

28

What we think about ourselves translates into how we interact with the world around us. We want to mirror the positive, healthy, joyous parts of the world back to us. Being kind starts with being kind to yourself.

NOW IT'S YOUR TURN!

I AM _____!

Use I AM statements throughout the day.
Write it. Say it. Sing it. Dance to it.

The most important thing is that you
BELIEVE it!

CELEBRATE BIG AND SMALL

Celebrate the small things. What may seem to be an easy task and no big deal to others may be a huge achievement for someone else.

Finn celebrates every time he completes a nail trim at his holistic vet. We call it a "Courage Day" and he beams with pride when he is done. Everyone around him celebrates it, too.

Imagine if we all did this for one other? Celebrating all our triumphs, big and small, together and cheering one another on, that is living in the MEOW!

Take a moment to think of all the amazing talents you possess and how you can share them with the world. What you do may change throughout time, but the important thing is to share those gifts in the MEOW. The world needs all of our gifts in order to thrive and bring good to others.

Share them!

Next
Wu Kitty book

Try to slow down. We are able to connect better with ourselves, others and our world when we are more focused, less rushed, more peaceful, less frustrated and much more appreciative of all we already have.

You see, my friends, like I said in the beginning, animals have no agenda and no worries, we don't get fixated on the past or worry about the future. We just are.

You can "JustB" too. Living in the MEOW.

Start now – find the nearest sunbeam and practice.

It's easy to "JustB" – just follow me!

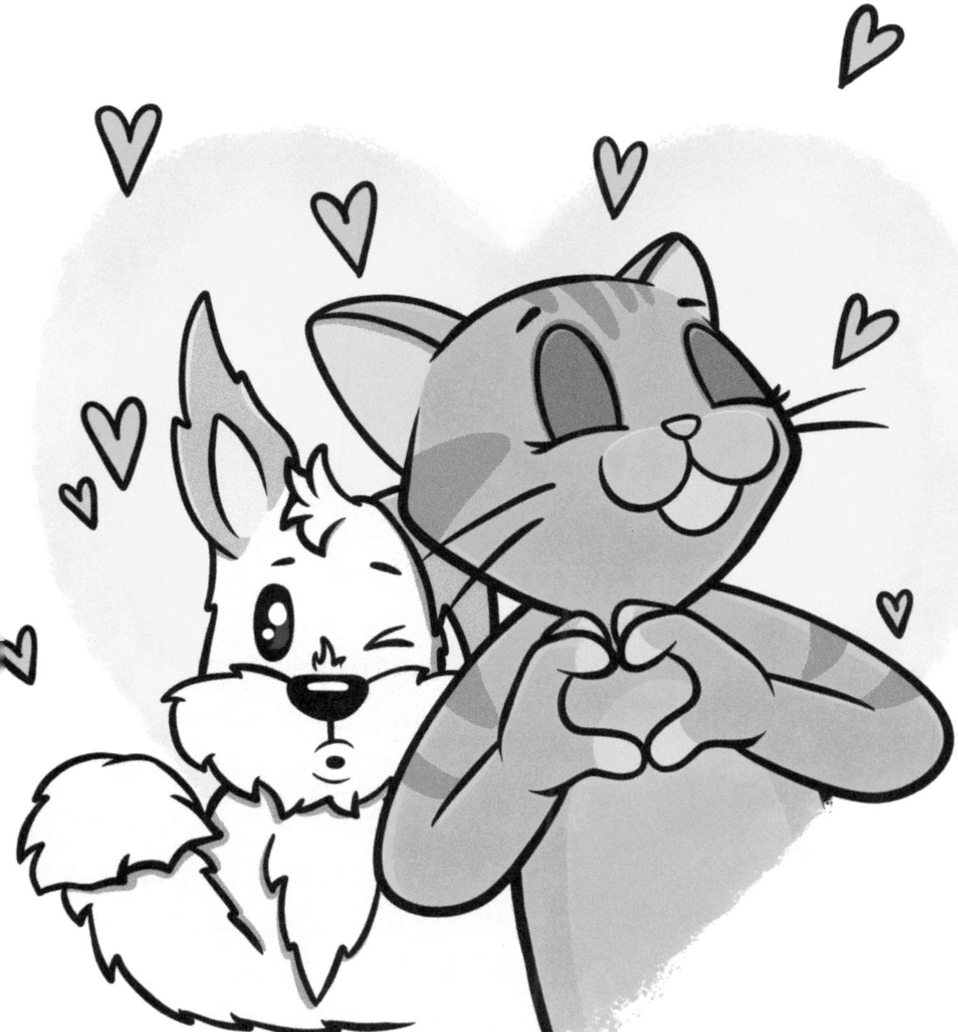

The End

About the Author

Originally from Cape Cod, Massachusetts, Kimberly Fleck is a small business owner, social media creator, author, podcaster, storyteller, autoimmune warrior, wellness activist and animal advocate. She holds a Master of Arts in special education and a Bachelor of Fine Arts, with minors in history and women's studies. She currently resides in Connecticut, where she lives with her rescue dog and rescue cats. At the core of Kimberly's being is her love of all animals and her passion around humane education and self-care. She's been a member of the Cat Writers' Association since 2017 and involved in animal rescue for decades. Learn more about her at brandfearless.com.

About the Illustrator

Born in Chicago, Illinois, Mexican-American illustrator Jessica Aranda is a self-taught artist. She currently resides in Indiana, where she lives with her husband of 18 years, Juan Pablo, their two children, Melanie and Angel, and their three dogs. Her passion for art grew stronger when she realized inspiration isn't something you think of, but something you feel. This feeling can be sensed behind every character she creates and she hopes to continue to spread this positive energy for years to come.

A portion of the proceeds from this
book will go to Boston's Forgotten Felines,
a 501(c)3 organization dedicated to caring
for the endless community and feral cats in
Boston, MA, and providing humane education
and community outreach.

Bostonsforgottenfelines.org

CPSIA information can be obtained
at www.ICGtesting.com
Printed in the USA
LVHW071248010921
696679LV00017B/97

9 781637 650509